R. Timothy Rush

A FULL CIRCLE

Professor Tim Rush teaches graduate and undergraduate courses in literacy education, humanities education, and linguistics at the University of Wyoming. Working closely with the tribes of the Wind River Indian Reservation, he has helped develop UW programs for certifying teachers of American Indian children. He was awarded the University of Wyoming Outreach School's Holon Family Award and was recognized by the International Reading Association with its Jerry Johns Outstanding Teacher Educator in Reading Award. Tim Rush lives on the high plains west of Laramie, Wyoming, with Alice, his wife of fifty years, and an array of horses, dogs, cats, and regular guests from the wild kingdom.

First published by GemmaMedia in 2017.

Gemma Open Door
230 Commercial Street
Boston MA 02109 USA

www.gemmamedia.org

Printed in the United States of America
978-1-936846-60-3

Photo courtesy of Burnett Lee Whiteplume, Ph.D.

Excerpt from *Dictionary of the Northern Arapaho Language (Revised)* © 1998, reprinted with permission.

Cover by Laura Shaw Design.

Gemma's Open Doors provide fresh stories, new ideas, and essential resources for young people and adults as they embrace the power of reading and the written word.

Brian Bouldrey
Series Editor

Open Door

This book is dedicated to all who
know and live this truth:
Good returns to those who do good.

Characters

The Arapaho

Neiwoo "NAY-wah" (Grandmother)—An independent old woman and the hero of her family.

Hiieeniibei "Hee-AN-ee-bay" (Sings in the Light)—Granddaughter of Neiwoo and teller of the story. Wise and fearless, she is ten or eleven years old.

Nowoo3 "Nah-WATH" (Left Hand)—Hiieeniibei's brother. He is a year or two older or younger than his sister.

Jade Stone—A mysterious green-eyed girl who sacrifices herself to save little children.

The Oglala Lakota

Tasina Sa "Tah-SEE-nah Sah" (Red Blanket)—A tall, pretty Lakota woman warrior.

Looking Glass—An Army scout and the partner of Tasina Sa.

The Norwegians

Arnulv Arentzen—Older of two bachelor brothers who emigrated from Norway.

Gunnar Arentzen—Like his brother, Gunnar takes great risks to help his friends and the children they protect.

A Full Circle

One morning, when I was a little boy, I sat between my mother and grandmother and listened to a very old Arapaho Indian woman tell a story. She sat across the table from us, sipping black coffee with a heavy woolen blanket around her shoulders.

The room was dark and smoky. She looked out the open door to a horse corral. There, my father stood talking with a very old man with long, white, braided hair. Between them stood a little gray horse named Flicka that would soon be mine.

"My brother is the horse tamer. Since he was a boy, horses have listened to him," she said. "When we were young, the Fort Bob soldiers saw this in him. That is why we two Arapahos live here today, in Oglala Lakota country."

She stood and refilled three coffee cups.

"But the story truly begins with another old woman and a great adventure we had when I was still a child . . ."

CHAPTER 1

1878
November
(Moon When the Leaves Fall Heavily)

My grandmother Neiwoo was sick the day that the Army's horse soldiers herded us from the valley village into the place they called Fort Robinson. We were with nineteen other very young or very old—and all very hungry—Arapaho and Oglala Lakota people.

Grandmother had fallen. Her head hurt. She was very weak and moved slowly. For two days, she had stumbled along between my brother—called Nowoo3, or Left Hand—and me. She had always been strong and spry. Now she seemed ancient. Everyone thought she would die. Everyone but I, Sings in the Light.

We looked down from a ridge at Fort Robinson, the cavalry post about a mile away. Grandmother whispered hoarsely, "*Niioo3o*" (nee-AW-tha). *Spider*. The White Man's place looked like a spider's web. Streets were the silk web. Big houses, tents, and wagons were the spider and its visitors. I did not want to walk down into the spider's web.

At "Fort Bob," as the soldiers called it, there were many other Indian people. Cheyenne and Lakota and Arapahos, like us. And like us, they were thin and shabby. But they were happy to see us. Neiwoo, brother, and I were given a small, awkward tent made of heavy, once-white Army canvas. It was hung on a frame of too few and too short wooden poles. Instead of bright story-paintings, only the big black letters *U.S.* were painted on its walls.

The tent was empty, except for a crazy long-necked iron box on legs. Compared to our own tall, graceful tents, this one was low, sharp-edged, and unfriendly. But after two days in the open, we had no complaints. We were grateful for any shelter.

Our people knew some of the Oglala Lakota women, who brought us things we needed from a big house on a low hill. The Oglala Lakota had lived at the old Red Cloud Indian Agency, near this "Fort Bob," for a long time. But then their brave young leader, Crazy Horse, was murdered. After that, almost all their people, and the Agency, were moved north of here, to a place called Pine Ridge Reservation.

The Oglala Lakota, along with the Northern Cheyenne tribe, were the Northern Arapaho tribe's oldest friends. Their languages sounded like ours—when we tried hard, we could talk to each other. For making our beds, these women gave us blankets and robes left behind in the big Agency warehouses. Of course, the Arapaho women helped us, too. But, like us, they had just been brought to Fort Bob. They had little they could give.

Over a fireplace outside, I boiled soup in a black iron kettle. That soup was mostly broth made from the boiled bones of White Man cattle. Then a tall young Oglala woman brought some stew meat and added it to the pot. It would make us warm and stronger and able to remember. Arapahos are famous for their strong memories.

Now we were helpless and hungry. But only two summers before, before the big Greasy Grass fight with Yellowhair Custer's Army, life had been good. True, for ten years before that, we'd had some fights with soldiers and Americans. But mostly our leaders stayed away from them. Our men and women warriors fought them bravely when fights could not be avoided. Some Arapahos had loved ones buried in secret places near Fort Bob. Loved ones including the parents of Left Hand and me.

When more and more Whites came, Neiwoo said we should "keep away from these Americans." So we had joined a little band of old people and young orphans and followed the young Warrior Woman and the young man Gentles Horses. They led us far into the empty ocean of grass.

They were beautiful together. They found the warm, secret valley and the little buffalo herd. For a year, we lived well near a hidden spring below the first mountains.

Then, one dark day, came the thunder of long rifles, and we found all the buffalo lying dead. Many Army horse soldiers came. Our two young leaders rode out to meet them. We saw them no more.

The next morning, soldiers herded us toward the rising sun. Behind us, the flames from our few pretty painted tipis sent black smoke into the sky. Only the soldiers rode. Our fine ponies were all shot down. We wept for them and Gentles Horses, who had tamed them while Left Hand watched in wonder.

Neiwoo, my brother, and I were all of our family who had survived the Sand Creek Massacres and the Indian Wars. Tonight, we huddled in the too-low tent whose doorway did not correctly face the rising sun. And we remembered the rich buffalo meat. Meat we had eaten with the young woman and young man warriors. There, in our tall, graceful lodges on the endless grasslands.

Nowoo3 brought some wood and

chips inside for the night. Friends had taught him how to make fire in the iron box he now called "stove." Neiwoo had thanked Creator for sustenance and fire.

I sat on the flattened-grass floor beside Neiwoo. I fed her with the big spoon from the pot. I took some for myself between her sips.

"Hiieeniibei (Hee-AN-ee-bay)," my grandmother murmured my name. "Your hands make excellent soup." Then she rolled her delicate brown face into the crook of my arm and slept.

In twenty other low, Army-canvas tents and a few Arapaho tipis, friends were with their families. They helped each other with fires, cooking, and laying out makeshift beds.

Soldiers in blue coats brought a

wagon filled with firewood and dried buffalo chips. They piled the fuel in the center of this circle of odd little tents with doorways that looked in the wrong directions.

CHAPTER 2

Fort Bob

I lay down beside Neiwoo, sharing her covers. Listening to her soft breathing, I fell asleep. We dreamed. She dreamed of the happy years of freedom in the tall grass with our people. Neiwoo held memories of her long life living in the old way.

But my dreams were restless. I woke up remembering our ponies falling and our village burning. Everything was suddenly so terrifying and uncertain. So cruel.

Grandmother stirred, needing to go outside. I helped her shuffle out and back. She lay down and I covered her again.

"Granddaughter," she whispered. "Tell me again a story of Warrior Woman."

I knew this was her way of distracting me from my bad dreams. It was also a kind of test. The more I told the story, the better I would remember it. I had listened to her tell it on many nights before. I think she knew that without the telling of the story, our people would forget that Arapaho and Oglala Lakota women once fought fiercely beside their men. Some, like Warrior Woman and Pretty Nose, were heroes and avengers. Maybe Neiwoo wanted me to be like them. Maybe she wanted all Arapaho women to be like them. I started the story:

"She was brave and strong. She rode and hunted and fought beside Fast

Horses, her brother. Each one saved the other in buffalo hunts and fights with the enemy. Like him, she was calm and fearless at all times. They made good luck together . . . right up to the end."

Grandmother smiled and sighed softly. "The bear story?"

I began. "When Warrior Woman and Fast Horses were young, they hunted game by waiting at dawn along trails where big animals traveled. Fast Horses took his deer first. He prayed thanks in the Arapaho way. Then he dressed out the deer where it had fallen to his arrow. Carefully, he separated the heart, liver, and other organs. These he placed inside the belly. He carried the deer to the trail, near the cliff wall. From there he could see that his sister had taken her deer, too.

Their family would have meat to share with others.

"As he took a step in her direction, he heard the monster and inhaled its scent at the same instant. Leaping from the trail and turning in midair, he saw the giant yellow bear tearing at his deer. Before his feet touched the ground, he sent an angry arrow deep into its shoulder.

"For long seconds, the bear seemed not to notice. It tore a mouthful from the deer's belly, then quickly stood tall. The bear roared the name of Fast Horses. That is what the boy thought.

"Fast Horses ran to the cliff wall and out along a narrow ledge. Fast Horses could wait here. The bear could not follow. There was no room. But the bear followed.

"The boy backed along the narrowing ledge of cold stone. To his left, the wall pushed against his shoulder. From his right came the echo of the river in the mists far below. In front of him, the snuffling, angry, yellow bear came closer and closer. The arrow in the creature's shoulder dripped blood into the white mists.

"The girl who would become Warrior Woman heard the roar and turned just in time to see everything. Quickly, she came to help her brother. Now, she drew her bow and let its arrow go. The monster bear gave a startled 'woof,' turned, and fell silently into eternity."

Neiwoo smiled and slept again.

Soon all three of us were sleeping.

CHAPTER 3

A Rumor

In the morning, we heard talk that in seven days the Army would move us and two hundred more of our Arapaho people to a new place in Wyoming Territory. Our chiefs, Sharp Nose and Black Coal, knew the place. They wanted to go there. It was green and well-watered. In winter, it was warm and sheltered from the wind. There was game of many kinds for our hunters. The Army wanted to take us to the south to Oklahoma Territory instead, but Washington said, "The Northern Arapahos go West."

Our cousins, the Southern Arapaho, had been taken to a reservation in the

Oklahoma Territory ten years before. Their reservation was shared with the Cheyenne people. It lay far to the south of our old homeland, which had been near the White Man town of Denver.

That afternoon, we saw Tasina Sa (Red Blanket), the tall, kind Oglala woman who had given us stew meat. She told us that the rumor was true. Her man was an Army scout and she knew a lot. We remaining Arapaho would live in Wyoming Territory with the Shoshone, our old enemies and new friends. The sick would be left behind. The Army doctor would give them White Man medicines from Fort Robinson. When the soldiers carried the Arapaho people and all they owned away to the unknown place, Grandmother would stay here—alone.

But Left Hand and I would not leave Neiwoo alone, and we told Tasina Sa so. Our healers knew the medicine herbs and roots and barks. These would make her quick and strong again. They knew, too, the prayers and songs.

We knew that Army forts held many sicknesses. We told our new friend that we must take Grandmother back to the valley by the hidden spring. Or we would smuggle her into a wagon and take her on the trip with us to Wyoming.

Tasina Sa knew the road through Wyoming Territory. She said she had a secret plan to help, but we must not ask or fuss. Just do as we were told.

Meanwhile, she prepared us to leave Neiwoo with her. Her man, Looking Glass, the scout, was away guiding some

Texas cowboys and their two thousand cattle to the Pine Ridge. The herd would reach Fort Bob tonight.

CHAPTER 4

Separation

That afternoon, we watched a braided Indian cowboy on a tough little Indian pony lead spotted longhorn cattle into the camp. Steers, calves, and cows trotted through a gate in a long line with cowboys on each side.

In the big corral, they watered at long tanks. Their long horns softly clicked together. Then they began to tear at piles of dry grass hay left for them on the ground. Soon they lay down to rest.

The next morning, all the cattle jumped to their feet. Four cowboys rode into the herd on quick little spotted ponies. Left Hand looked at grandmother and me. "They are like our ponies," he said, and smiled.

Moving slowly, the ponies forced some of the younger cattle away from the rest. The cowboys shouted and whistled. Their ponies crowded this little pod of half-grown cattle toward a smaller corral on the far side of the fort. We could tell the cows in the big herd did not want to be separated from the others. They stood looking between the rails of the tall wooden fence and bawled. The young ones bawled and tried turning back to their mothers. The little ponies blocked them and moved them farther and farther away.

Grandmother turned from the sight. Her face was dark and troubled.

CHAPTER 5

A Long Way to Walk

Seven days passed, and the soldiers and contractors gathered the Arapaho people. "Just like those cows," someone said. The Americans loaded the old and the very young into big, mule-drawn covered wagons. Other wagons carried tents, blankets, food, and supplies. Army horse soldiers guided twenty wagons as they started off. Two hundred Indians followed on foot. The weak sun of early November warmed our backs.

Some people joked: "We look like a train of White Man wagons heading west. We better watch out for

Redskins!" They laughed. Arapahos are great jokesters.

I looked over my shoulder. I remembered about Tasina Sa's "plan" and did not fight or try to run back to Neiwoo. The soldiers would easily catch me. I did not want to make trouble for my people. So I sang Neiwoo's old songs as I rode along in the great, rumbling wagon. The arched canvas covering made it seem like riding inside a giant drum. I could hardly hear my own voice.

The weak sun would rise twelve times before we reached the new place. At the end of each day, we prepared a meal and made our beds in or under the wagons. No time was taken to put up tents.

The first night on the road was confused. Everything was muddled. Women hunted through wagons for cooking pots, ladles, and spoons. Men rolled out blankets and robes that had been thrown into wagons helter-skelter. Children and old ones were everywhere. Soldiers on horses came and went.

And—that herd of half-grown cattle from Fort Bob appeared behind us. The herd was a jumble of motion in a thick fog of dust, but two braided Indian cowboys seemed to be moving the cattle. A low supply wagon bumped along a little distance behind them.

When it was time to eat, Nowoo3 and I were taking our heaping bowls to the place under a wagon where we had made our sleeping pallets. A braided cowboy leaned over and nudged me toward the open tailgate of the wagon.

I looked up—Tasina Sa! In the Indian way, she pointed into the wagon with her chin. Neiwoo smiled from the shadows!

Tasina Sa was one of the cowboys with the little herd! Brother and I knew then that our grandmother had hidden in the wagon. We looked at the tall Oglala woman with new respect and gratitude. That night we would talk long after others slept.

CHAPTER 6

A Winter of No Wind

Our train of wagons and people and four-leggeds moved steadily. The White men and the Indians knew that winter would return to catch us any day. We wanted to be sheltered when it came.

There was no complaining. We remembered. Each night, our people told of moves we had made in the old times when we followed the buffalo. The times when we moved from summer to winter camps in sheltered places. Places so cold that trees popped like gunshots in the night. And we talked about moves to summer camps in the cool, breezy highlands.

The White Man road we followed was smooth, straight, and hard. Fort Robinson to Fort Casper and west to Shoshoni. Then we turned south, toward the place where the Big and Little Wind Rivers meet. All the while, Tasina Sa and Looking Glass trailed along with the herd of little White Man cattle.

Twice we crossed wide rivers. At Fort Casper there was a floating bridge called a ferry. Our elders knew of places to walk across that river. But the Army men did not use those ways. At the Wind River, there was no ferry, and we did ride and walk across. On the other side lay the place that would be our new home.

The new place was like all the old places where Arapahos had made their villages. There was good water, breezy high ground away from the water and biting flies, and grass for horses, cattle, and game animals. But there was nothing else.

We started life in Wyoming Territory with only the things we had brought from Nebraska. We would have to survive as we always had—by hunting and gathering and learning new ways.

At first we lived in the little U.S. tents, but our men and boys found stands of lodgepole pine trees. Choosing trees as tall as three men, they cut down the best and brought them to our new place. Then they stripped the trees of branches and bark, down to pure white wood. In teams of men and boys, they stood the poles up and lashed them to make frames for our graceful Arapaho lodges.

I helped Neiwoo and other women cut and sew the U.S. canvas to make coverings for the frames. They were not the same as old-time buffalo-hide covers. Yet they protected us from the snow and wind. It was not long before life seemed almost good again.

CHAPTER 7

Cowboys

We all were busy and winter passed quickly. None of us children could remember a time before the Army had chased us—a time when we could stay put in winter.

As trees budded and grass sprouted, we young ones found time for games and learning useful skills. Grandmothers and aunties taught us girls about butterflying and drying meat. We watched and learned about tanning animal skins. We decorated hides with beads, quills, teeth, and bone.

Boys learned to make tools of hunting. They also made flutes and drums for ceremonies and dances. The young ones sat listening and watching the hands of their grandfathers and uncles. The children imitated the movements of their elders.

There was laughter in our village and good stories when our hunters returned with game.

After spending the winter with us, the soldiers and our Lakota friends headed back to Fort Robinson, following their slow-moving wagons. Promising to bring more cattle, Tasina Sa and Looking Glass left the small herd and a few remount horses and mules with us. We became Indian cowboys.

CHAPTER 8

1879
Neiwoo's Dream

The morning that Tasina Sa and the soldiers left us, Neiwoo was missing from our lodge. I found her watching our Arapaho cowboys gather cattle by the river. She sat on a slope above the riverbank. There was a dark expression on her face.

"Something is wrong, grandmother?" I asked. She started a little and looked up. Then she patted the ground beside her. I sat down. "I am worried, granddaughter. I had a bad dream."

I sat and waited for her to begin. "Do you remember the herd of many cattle at Fort Bob?" she asked in a low voice. I nodded, yes.

"The cows and calves were together, resting after their long trail." She drew a circle on the ground with the end of a stick, then poked many dots inside the circle. "Then the cowboys rode in and took the little ones away from their mothers."

We remembered the bawling of the mothers and the calves. "All through the night, they called to each other." Neiwoo winced. "They would never see each other again."

"Yes, I am still sad for them—the babies and the mothers. They were helpless," I replied. "Was this your dream?"

"Much worse. My dream was that the men rode into our camp with horses and wagons to take our young ones. Not our cattle. Our children!" Her face became both fearful and angry. "They took our children. You and Left Hand. We were like the cows. You were the calves. We could do nothing." She drew a breath and set her jaw. "I have lost my children to the White Man wars. I will not lose my two grandchildren."

That night, Neiwoo told her dream to others around the campfire and there was much talk. Others had heard of this White Man practice from families in the Indian Territories. Their children were being taken to faraway places called "boarding schools" to be made into White people.

Others said, "Don't worry. We are far away from our cousins in the south.

Look at the faces around you. What school could make us White?" Everyone laughed. But not Neiwoo.

Yet only the next day news came that Taker Men were close by. The very night before, four children had been taken from their families to a place called Carlisle. The children cried for their mothers, fathers, grandmas, and grandpas. There was no kindness shown. The men had pistols and rifles and they threatened families. These people knew they had to cooperate. Men with government badges and guns could punish. The badges meant the guns would be used.

One boy of eight summers escaped the Taker wagon and ran away and was home again before the sun was overhead. He said that the men and wagon were headed south, to the iron railroad. The boy was honored for his cleverness, but an hour later, one of the riders appeared and took him again. This time, the boy slumped in the saddle before the rider. He listened to his family's grief as he was carried off. He did not return. Now we knew we could be next to see the Taker Men.

Neiwoo did not hesitate. She stood tall, saying, "We go back to Nebraska, to the hidden canyon below the White Buttes!" Her back was straight. Her voice was hard as stone. No more was she the frail old woman who stumbled into Fort Robinson last summer.

At sunset, we were ready to leave. I was afraid and wanted to start. Instead, we rested for our journey.

CHAPTER 9

Taken

The eastern sky was turning gray when shouting *niioo3o* voices woke everyone in our little tipi village. There were three men in blue with black hats and boots. All had Winchesters cradled in their arms and six-shooters holstered at their hips.

A fourth Taker, who was not a man, rumbled up our bumpy road in a big covered wagon like the ones that had brought us to Wyoming. She had a shiny black bullwhip coiled over one knee. Everyone looked her way when the wagon stopped. She nodded. Her face was stern, but her eyes were kind.

Her frame was strong. She had the look of a White Arapaho woman.

A big Taker Man was talking quietly with our elder, Oldman, in something like Arapaho mixed with American and sign. He looked like one of the soldiers who had ridden with us from Fort Robinson.

Oldman was angry, but the White Man raised his voice and shifted his rifle. Then Oldman spoke the words we feared: "These men are taking children who have four to twelve summers away to live at their school. Our young ones will be warm and have plenty to eat. They will learn White Man ways and bring them back to the People." Oldman tried to smile.

This meant that Left Hand and I were

caught. Brother ran into the high sagebrush to get away. I could see his head bobbing above the leaves as he ran. The leader shouted, and seven helper Indians on horseback appeared from below the horizon. My brother dodged, but it was no use. Left Hand came back jogging between two dark-skinned horsemen.

We and four little ones from our camp were walked to the wagon. Inside were five young children and a pretty girl who seemed about eleven summers old—the same age as me.

We did not have time to eat or say proper goodbyes to our families. Grandmother came to the tailgate and said she would pray and be with us always. She said she was sorry we had waited. Her eyes flashed a signal that said, "I will come for you."

The Taker Men had jerky and dry meat in their wagon. They gave this to us as the wheels began to turn. We older ones held the young ones close. It would be a four-day journey to the railroad station in the town called Medicine Bow.

Along the way, we learned that there were other men and wagons moving across the Wind River Reservation, taking the children from other families. To us older ones, it seemed our world was truly ending. I don't know what the small ones felt—besides fear and confusion.

The wagon droned along, stopping twice before we came to a place where we were fed a meal of soup and heavy fried bread. The two mules that had followed the wagon were harnessed and brought forward to pull. Their sweat-stained partners took their places behind the wagon. Anytime we came to water, every two- and four-legged creature drank.

CHAPTER 10

To Medicine Bow

The pretty girl was named Jade Stone, and along the way we became friends. I began to think she was older than me, and older than she looked. She had a very gentle way with the young ones. All of them took to her naturally. Three, in particular, seemed to be her favorites. Once she hushed the smallest of those three after the little girl called her "mama" in our language. The pretty girl's green eyes told me to be quiet. I did. I guessed her secret.

The third night, one of the men sneaked into our wagon and pushed himself at Jade Stone. I cried out and kicked at him hard. As I tried to help my friend, a strong arm reached past me, and the man was lifted into the air and thrown from the wagon. The person with the strong arm followed him, like a shadow. There was a short fight and the man lay still in the dirt. The strong Taker Woman came back to us and signed that we would be safe now.

As we traveled the next day, I sat looking back over the tailgate. Late in the day, my eyes imagined that they saw puffs of dust on the far horizon. This happened three times.

CHAPTER 11

Tasina Sa and Looking Glass

Neiwoo did not rest. She would later tell me that as soon as Nowoo3 and I were taken, she began to walk for help. She followed the soldiers and our Oglala friends. The miles were many, but her pace was fast. She traveled faster than the wagons. At the end of the first day, she caught up with them.

Tasina Sa was ready to ride to Medicine Bow. Looking Glass, too.

The soldier captain and his men had come to like and respect the Arapaho during their winter together. He understood their feelings about kidnapping. So he ordered that his strongest remount horses be "loaned" to his Indian scout and the two women. They left well before sunset.

Leading two Army horses, lightly packed with rations and bedrolls, the three rode south on two stout little Indian ponies and a tall bay American horse. Before they rested, they were between the towns of Casper and Medicine Bow, at the site of the Bates Hole battle. By the end of the next day, they began to scan the prairie for wagon dust.

Before dawn on the third morning since the kidnapping, the Taker Men and their wagon came into view. They were still camped.

Neiwoo and the Oglala couple talked about different rescue plans as they rode. The safest way was to sneak in at night and spirit the children silently away. Neiwoo said it would be as easy as stealing enemy horses in the old times.

"But once they are re-stolen from the Takers," asked Tasina Sa, "how do we bring them back home to their people?" Then she added, "There are nine or ten children, mostly little. What if the rescue works? How far can we all travel without them being caught again?"

As his partner finished, Looking Glass exclaimed, "The Arentzen brothers! Their place is less than half a day south of the Medicine Bow station. They are kind and will help us. If one of us rides to the Arentzen place, they will come in their stagecoach."

Neiwoo and Tasina Sa agreed to the plan. As they moved toward the railroad, Looking Glass told them about the brothers. "When they were boys, the four brothers came from across the Atlantic water to help build the railroad. At Laramie, one brother was killed, and the youngest was taken in a raid by Red Cloud's fighters. The other two brothers stayed near Laramie to look for the little brother. They still search."

Neiwoo had known this story, but not the names of the brothers. She agreed that they were strong, brave, and kind, and that they would help with the rescue.

CHAPTER 12

Escape and Surrender

The plan worked. The night was windy, making it hard to hear and see. The three White men and their woman leader slept on the ground, wrapped deep in their blankets.

Neiwoo and Tasina Sa woke brother and me. We woke Jade Stone and silently brought out the small ones. We crossed the sagebrush-dotted red earth. We were concealed by drifting clouds of dust.

The way south offered many dry washes where even the horses could walk unseen. In one of these, the little party moved as swiftly as could be. Looking Glass mounted his best pony and loped off toward the Arentzen brothers' ranch. He skirted the little town of Rock Creek, crossed the railroad, and was welcomed at the ranch by noon.

Neiwoo and the rest of us were to walk to the Rock Creek crossing and wait in the brush near the road. We had the Army food that had been packed on the spare horses. We found a creek that ran fast with cool water.

We were near the creek when Left Hand looked above the rim of the wash and saw the Takers come into view. For a moment, panic stopped my breath. We had four good horses, but there were too many of us to ride, even two or three on a horse.

It happened so fast! Jade Stone, a woman who seemed a girl, spoke like a chief. “My children and I go back to the Takers. They took us from nothing. We have no home and no people. I go with them to the new place where we will have food and each other. I can be sure my children will not forget our people’s ways.”

The pretty young woman helped us mount the horses and watched us ride away. Then, she boosted her three young ones to the edge of the arroyo. They began to walk through the wind-driven dust clouds toward the Takers.

CHAPTER 13

We Ride to Safety

Neiwoo and the rest of us rode to the river. Then we followed it until it met a wagon road. We forded there.

On the far side of the river, Tasina Sa recognized the hoofprints of her man's pony, and we followed the tracks. The sun was beginning to rise, so we walked beside the road to be harder to see. We feared we would be followed. Jade Stone and her children had turned back to the Takers. But still, we worried.

Tasina Sa, her head tilted downward, guided her pony to follow Looking Glass's tracks. She rode like this for miles before she turned her pony west on a two-track road. We could see that it led toward a splotch of green in the yellow grass at the base of a long mountain.

The mountain was one that Neiwoo knew from the old times. "This long mountain is a sacred place to our people," she said with awe in her voice. "Many Faces Mountain. Far to its south end is the white-rock offerings place. Over there"—she turned her face to point north—"there is the Moon Mesa, where all the People gathered to pray. When I was a girl—when the buffalo were many and the White men were few."

Then, from the green place between our little group and the sacred mountain, we saw a boxlike wagon and two riders turn onto our path. They hurried toward us.

The riders hardly slowed when they reached us. One of the brothers stopped the wagon and turned it around. Neiwoo helped the small children off our horses and into the wagon bed and climbed up with them. We tied two of our Army horses to the wagon, and one of the Arentzens drove it back to the ranch. He urged his four-horse team to pull hard and fast. Left Hand and I hurried to keep up.

Tasina Sa shouted to the stage driver, "Hide them! Bounty hunters coming!" Then she whirled her little pony and nearly flew after the other Arentzen brother and Looking Glass.

They reined in their horses and stopped on a rise. Looking into the distance, they saw no one following. There,

Tasina Sa told the others how one of the "children" had taken a few small ones back to the Takers so that the rest could escape.

CHAPTER 14

Arentzen Springs

After half an hour, the three riders began trotting toward the ranch. Their path took them through many reddish, white-faced cattle. They rode straight through the yellow grasses to a small cabin in the greening poplar trees.

There, a long, low barn stood at one end of an open yard. It seemed like an arbor where Arapahos might hold dances and ceremonies. There were some fences, but it was not as much like a spider web as Fort Robinson. The stagecoach stood concealed inside the wide barn's entrance.

Inside the cabin, we travelers

were finishing our second bowls of "Norwegian stew." Arnulv Arentzen knew how to make stew.

As we finished eating, we children began to look around the cabin. The little ones looked with eyes drowsy from missed sleep. A roof with no smoke hole was a new thing for us, but we were tired. Soon all except Left Hand and I were snoring softly.

Cabins were not new to our rescuers. Tasina Sa and Looking Glass seemed not to notice the walls and roof around and above them. They talked and signed with the brothers, words something like these:

"If they come, they might use their guns," said Gunnar Arentzen. "There is the matter of bounty money lost."

"Yes," replied his brother. "For each

Indian child brought in, the United States pays fifty dollars, I think. More than a man can make for working sixty days on the railroad."

Hearing about bounty money for the first time, Tasina Sa, Looking Glass, and Neiwoo gave each other startled looks. Anger burned in my grandmother's eyes. Now she understood. Indian children were being stolen for profit.

The brothers began to make a plan. Would Looking Glass and Tasina Sa help them move a herd of white-faced cattle to Nebraska? If Takers were met along the way, the brothers would pay the Takers fifty dollars each to keep the Arapaho children free. Maybe they would meet no Takers. If so, the ransom money would be offered to Tasina Sa and

Looking Glass. It would pay for herding the cattle and guiding the travelers.

Arnulv noticed Left Hand perk up, and he said, "If the boy can ride and work cows, we pay him, too." He hesitated, then added, "Not so much though, maybe." He chuckled at his joke. I laughed because I knew my brother wanted to sign that he would ride for free.

"But here is the thing," said Gunnar. "In the big coach, we bring the little children on the drive to Crawford in Nebraska. We get them to their people there. Too many bounty hunters at Wyoming Reservation now. So, we go around them."

Gunnar continued. "But right now, we can expect to see horse soldiers come looking for these children, so we must hide them."

"We have the barn loft and root cellars, but those are like hiding in plain sight. Soldiers and bounty hunters look in these first," added his older brother, Arnulv.

Neiwoo was listening. Now, she stood and signed, "There is a secret door in the mountain here."

The Arentzen brothers gave each other looks of surprise. Arnulv spoke first, to Looking Glass. "What did she say? Secret door? No. Not around here." Gunnar confirmed there was no such place. The brothers knew every inch of this land, even outside the boundaries of the sections they owned.

But Neiwoo signed again. "You know

the Medicine Wheel on that mesa?" She nodded to the north. "You know the stairway leading up? The offerings stone? The stone arrows pointing the way?"

The brothers' faces went blank. The Lakota couple gulped air loudly and leaned on the backs of their White Man chairs, smiling.

Neiwoo smiled wisely and signed. "Come, I will show you."

CHAPTER 15

The Door in the Mountain

The brothers, Tasina Sa, and Looking Glass stood. Leaving me and Left Hand with the young ones, they followed Neiwoo out through the trees and onto the grasses.

Neiwoo looked high up the mountainside, and then off to the south. Then, angling upslope, she started walking with a purpose. None of the others could see what she was heading for—they saw only a high rock wall. At the cliff's base, water sprang up, flowed a short distance, and disappeared under the ground. The footing became rocky, and the followers stumbled as they trotted to keep up. Neiwoo never missed a step.

Not more than four hundred yards from the cabin in the woods, they watched the old woman disappear. She had just crossed the ranch boundary marker. One second she was in full view. The next second she was gone. Just as they started to run to where she had fallen, Neiwoo reappeared, standing tall with her arms folded across her chest.

Speechless, the brothers and their Indian friends came to the old woman's side. They found her standing on a brushy little hill that hid an arch in the rock wall. She led them through the arch.

The two Lakota rescuers had heard stories of this place. Like a stone house, it had walls all around. The overhanging cliff made the place open to the sky's light, but not to rain or snow. Summer birds nested here in every season. Chokecherries and other berries grew here, summer and winter. A gurgling spring pool held warm water and small fish.

Most important for Neiwoo and the children, the door in the wall was invisible to anyone who did not know it was here.

For long minutes, the Arentzen brothers could not stop exploring this grotto with their eyes. Then, they talked and agreed with Tasina Sa, Neiwoo, and Looking Glass. We children would live here with Neiwoo until it was time to drive the white-faced cattle north.

CHAPTER 16

Soldiers and Takers

Seven days after Neiwoo and we young ones moved through the door in the wall, soldiers came with two bounty-hunting Takers.

A captain and six soldiers rode in on tall brown horses from Fort Sanders at Laramie. The officer knew the Arentzen brothers and talked with them in friendly tones.

"We have been sent out to look for six Arapaho children who ran away from these bounty hunters on their way to boarding school," the officer explained. "They are all young. If they are alone, they are probably dead by now. These people want to be sure—they get paid for kids who they put on the train to Pennsylvania."

Arnulv asked the captain why the Army was looking for these children. "New law in Washington says that Indian children have to be taken completely away from their tribes and 'civilized' in White ways," the captain replied. "No home culture. No language. No tribe. No family. Something about 'killing the Indian to save the man.' Heartless cruel, but it is law."

Arnulv and Gunnar agreed about the cruelty, but said nothing about the Arapaho children they were protecting.

"We won't bother you fellows much," said the captain. "But we have to look around your place. Those are our orders."

"Sure, you go ahead. If there are any children on this place, we don't know about them," assured Arnulv.

While the captain talked with the brothers, the eyes of the Takers never stopped searching for signs of Indian children.

And, just as the captain and the Arentzens said goodbye, two braided Indians rode in from the big cow pasture. The Takers hefted their Winchesters.

The captain nodded, and his burly sergeant spurred his mount up close to the bounty hunters. "Easy now, friends. The war with these people is over. The law protects them now—at least the grown-ups," he added sarcastically. The Taker Men scowled, but rested their rifles.

The Arentzens told the captain in

loud voices that this man and woman worked for them and had come to help move three hundred white-faced Hereford cows and steers to a ranch over Nebraska way.

In fact, the big sergeant knew Looking Glass from when the Indian had scouted for the cavalry during the last of the Indian wars. He told the captain he liked and trusted this Indian.

The soldiers and the Takers were satisfied that Looking Glass and Tasina Sa worked on the ranch. They searched the barn and root cellars, then trotted their horses around the meadows for half an hour. From a distance, the soldiers saluted their goodbyes and loped away down the lane toward Laramie and Fort Sanders.

CHAPTER 17

Floating Mesa

We all knew it was time to go north with the cattle, but Neiwoo begged for a day. She needed to teach her grandchildren and the rest about this holy place. We would walk to the south end of the long mountain and back.

Seeing this was important to Neiwoo. Everyone agreed. We would start in the morning. The Arentzens and Looking Glass would ride along behind to guard.

"But for now," said Grandmother, "the Medicine Wheel. Come, we climb to the floating mesa."

It was a short walk to the foot of the mesa. After that, it was so steep that we had to climb on hands and knees. The stony slope was slippery, but we reached the flat top in an hour. As we stood and caught our breath, we saw stones laid out. A giant circle with spokes leading to a smaller circle in the middle. The ancient image of a wagon wheel from a time before any Indian had seen such a thing.

We walked along the flat mesa and found the outline of an arrow, laid out to point northward. Neiwoo said that there were many of these in places where plains tribes lived. She did not know why they were there. "Each one seems to point to another one," she said thoughtfully.

The next morning, we walked along the base of the long mountain. Neiwoo explained that this was called Many

Faces Mountain because when people looked at this peak from far away, they could see the outlines of giant faces looking up into the sky.

After many miles, Neiwoo tapped my hand and gestured with her chin. Ahead, we could see a low outcrop of dazzling white rock. When we moved closer, we could see the white stone was pocked with hundreds of small holes. Closer still, we could see that someone had left little treasures in the holes.

From her rawhide parfleche box, Neiwoo took a small, finely beaded buckskin bag. She began a song as she placed it in a high, empty pocket in the white stone. Her song was a prayer for our safety.

CHAPTER 18

Jade Stone

Many years later, I learned the story of what had happened to Jade Stone—and of what had nearly happened to me.

Jade Stone and her young ones walked bravely toward the three Takers. At first the Whites did not see her through the flying red dust. Then they rode up quickly, took hold of the little ones, and put them up on saddles. The Takers climbed up behind them and turned back toward their camp. Jade Stone took hold of a horse's long tail and walked with them.

At the camp, the Takers were angry at each other. "Four of us and ten kids walk away in a dust storm! If it weren't for the bounty, I would wish the little skunks dead," yelled the big man.

"Tom, are you blaming simple Indian brats for our stupidity?" chided the strong woman as she stirred a soup of potatoes, canned beans, and meat. "We might not find the others in a week of looking, and we have a train to meet."

Jade Stone understood just a little of the Americans' language, but she sensed that her friends and their children were safe.

She did not know how this could be. She prayed *hohou*, a word of thanks to Creator. She sang her prayer softly to her children.

Late in the day, the wagon stopped at a small house beside the railroad. White people stood around in small groups. Jade Stone was allowed to take the children into a tiny building and show them how an outhouse was used. Then they were led behind the tall house to a rough table with benches attached. Bowls and spoons were set out for them. They ate a mixture of something like bread, beans, and meat. They were given water that was clear, but smelled bad. They were hungry and thirsty and ate quickly.

As they finished, a short, kindly-looking man and a tall, stern-looking woman followed the strong Taker Woman to their table. Taker Woman talked to the children in Arapaho and sign. "Mister Wesson and Miss Smith will go with you on the train. In five days you will be at your new home."

The young children crowded around Jade Stone. She said not to worry in the Arapaho language. Mister Wesson smiled. But Miss Smith scowled and said, "English only!" She was talking to Wesson, but it was loud enough for all to hear.

Then she said to the children, "Come! We walk." She marched them off to the little house beside the rails.

The Arapaho children cowered next to Jade Stone while the new man and woman talked with Taker Woman. They handed some papers to her and she touched the papers with a white feather. Then, as the smoky locomotive came into view, she returned to the wagon.

The Takers sat and waited. Soon, they watched Wesson, White, four confused

Northern Arapaho children, and twenty more frightened young Indians roll toward the East. They left in a jail-car with bars on its windows. Kidnapped.

The train rocked and rolled, clicked and clacked on its way. Soon, the children were asleep around Jade Stone. She dozed, praying that all would be well for her children and for her friends Sings in the Light and Left Hand. She prayed, too, for the new faces that were drawn to her in their loneliness.

CHAPTER 19

On the Trail

Looking Glass was frustrated. He was used to herding Texas longhorn cattle that ran like deer. "These white-face cows are fat and slow and lazy!" he complained. "It will take the whole summer to move them three hundred miles to Crawford."

"Yes," replied Gunnar Arentzen, "but each one will feed ten people. One longhorn will feed two." He exaggerated, but the Herefords were far meatier than the longhorns.

The herd and crew of four riders had been on the trail for Fort Robinson for three days and had traveled barely fifteen miles.

The brothers had chosen to follow old, meandering wagon trails in order to keep out of sight; the Arapaho children would be attractive to bounty hunters and anyone else who had heard about stealing Indian children for boarding schools.

At first, the children were passengers in the big stagecoach. "You kids, you stay out of sight," Arnulv Arentzen gestured his warning. Left Hand and I made sure they understood. They listened—the rumbling Taker wagon would always be fresh in our minds.

After we crossed the rails and had followed the River Laramie for a day, old Arnulv felt sorry for us. He signed,

"Okay, you kids get down and walk. You big kids. You watch the little ones—don't let them fall behind or get lost. Grandma will watch you all." Blushing, he smiled at Neiwoo.

For a while, our job was easy. Every Arapaho child could walk faster than these red cattle with white-blazed faces. Then, in a canyon, the riders began to hear the snake-buzz in the grasses. We loaded into the coach and studied the walls of the canyon on one side and the fast-running creek on the other.

High on the steep walls were mountain sheep and goats. Unless they moved, they looked like gray stones. We saw a moose and her calf wading in the creek. She looked like a big horse. The little one was like a big dog.

Neiwoo told us that Arapaho used to share this place with our Cheyenne and Lakota cousins in the days before the White Man invaded. Her face was angry. But then she softened as she looked out at the brothers who were helping us now.

CHAPTER 20

A Gift with Horses

We followed the cattle and riders out of the canyon's mouth. Soon the rattlesnake sounds went away. We got down and walked along the bank of the stream. When the sun was high above, the riders stopped to eat and rest.

The men took out tobacco and lit smokes. They talked and laughed at jokes they told in Arapaho and American.

Old Arnulv got up from sitting cross-legged on the ground and groaned as he straightened his legs. "Uffda! Not used to all this riding and sitting on the hard ground." Then he walked into the willows above the creek.

When Arnulv returned, he talked straight to Left Hand. "You, boy. You go bring that little gray horse over to me." Left Hand hopped to his feet. I could see he was excited, but he walked slowly to the horse. He rubbed its neck with one hand. He reached down with the other to loosen the rope hobbles from the animal's legs.

My brother took the lead rope. The gray horse followed him like an old friend. Arnulv looked around smiling at Neiwoo and the other grownups. He took the rope, looped it over the horse's neck, and tied it at the bottom of the halter. "Okay, boy," he said, taking my brother by the arm. "Up you go! Flicka will take care of you."

Before he knew it, Left Hand was

a rider—and a cowboy. He took turns in the saddle with Arnulv, Tasina Sa, and the others. Left Hand never tired of cattle and horses, especially horses. Gunnar and Looking Glass taught him to use the lasso—something he would have learned from uncles and grandfathers in the old days. My brother suddenly seemed grown to a man.

Neiwoo and Tasina Sa wanted me to ride like Left Hand and they could. So I got lessons from them and Looking Glass. Soon I was riding beside my brother while we did the job of moving cattle. Together we crossed streams and pushed through swarms of mosquitoes and black flies. For twenty days, we forgot about Taker Men and wagons and our pretty green-eyed friend.

As we crossed the Niobrara River, trouble found us. It was not men who stole Indian children. This time, it was men who took cattle.

CHAPTER 21

Rustlers

Looking Glass and Left Hand had ridden ahead to mark our trail into Crawford, the White Man town beside Fort Robinson. From there, a rancher named Crouse and his crew would bring the herd to their new range.

Our scouts met a U.S. Mail wagon and asked the drivers to tell Crouse we were three days out of Crawford to the southwest.

When they returned to the herd, they saw twelve aimless riders who seemed to have no business loafing beside the trail.

Looking Glass knew this meant trouble and moved behind cover. There, the twelve riders could not see him and Left Hand. “Boy. One of us has to ride for help. You remember that mail wagon?” He spoke fast. “Ride to it. Then ride straight down the road to Fort Robinson. You have learned some American talk on this drive. You say this to the mail drivers and Army men: ‘Help. Army. Crouse. Rustlers. Hole in the Wall. Looking Glass.’” He made Left Hand repeat the words three times, then he slapped Flicka on the hip, spurred his pony, and both riders galloped in opposite directions.

“This is bad,” said Gunnar. “We can’t fight that many rustlers, and we have the kids. Those men would take them and sell them, too.”

“What is best to do?” his older brother asked.

"Left Hand brings help," Tasina Sa reminded them. "We should ride toward the help, that way." She looked in the direction that Looking Glass had just come.

So we moved on, pushing the cattle at a quicker pace. Gunnar guided the coach to the smoothest, fastest ground. We stayed alert for bad men.

CHAPTER 22

An Unlikely Posse

There was confusion at the fort. Since the fighting with the Sioux had ended, only a small number of soldiers remained. But there were still three hundred Arapaho waiting to be sent to Wyoming—or somewhere else, if the government could decide.

The mail wagon and the boy arrived. Left Hand reported that outlaws from the Hole in the Wall were going to steal a herd of prize beef cattle. The young lieutenant in charge could not decide what to do. Luckily, his burly sergeant stepped in.

The sergeant rode with the boy to the Arapaho leaders to ask for help. Left Hand described the cattle drive, the rescued children, and the outlaws.

Chief Black Coal wanted to help, but he had no horses. The sergeant said the Army had many in the big corral nearby. He instructed the soldiers to help the Arapaho. Then he and the boy hurried back to the lieutenant to explain the plan.

In half an hour, twenty unarmed Arapaho warriors thundered up to the little group of soldiers. The Arapaho leader nodded *wohei* ("Well done") to Left Hand.

"Can this boy show us the way?" The young lieutenant wanted to know.

The sergeant pointed to Left Hand and replied, "He can. He has traveled most of the distance twice this day."

The lieutenant shouted the order: "All right, troopers. Columns of twos. At-the-trot. Forward. Yo!"

And off they went. Eight blue coats rode in formation. Twenty Arapaho fighters, women and men, trotted on big, brown American horses, singing a war song. Before many miles had passed, the blue-coated soldiers were singing along.

CHAPTER 23

The Best Light Cavalry

The dozen outlaws were closing in. Not a shot had been fired, but we could see that the bad men had their guns ready. At shouting distance, they stopped. One man trotted forward and called out.

"We will be taking your herd," were his almost friendly words. "You just stand back out of the way."

Gunnar Arentzen and Looking Glass rode forward to meet him. Gunnar replied, "What can you do with these cattle? The law will know they are not yours."

The outlaw leader and his men chuckled. "We sell the cows, just like you. Crouse wants them. He will pay us just the same as he would pay you."

A second outlaw under a big black hat rode up to the leader. He leaned over in his saddle to say something. The black hat man looked familiar to me. A Taker Man!

"Oh, and when we are done with the beeves, we will have those heathen brats hiding in the coach," the outlaw leader said. There was ice in his voice this time. Then he waved an arm and six of his men fanned out to encircle the herd. The others drew pistols and rode for the coach.

Arnulv Arentzen slumped in his driver's seat. Until now it had seemed the children would be safe. "Everything now is lost," he seemed almost to sob. "We protect the little ones." He looked down at the shotgun between his feet.

And then, just as hope was gone, there was muffled thunder on the ridge above us. Down swooped a screaming band of Arapaho cavalry and blue-coated horse soldiers in full battle cry!

The outlaws scrambled like rabbits in every direction. The rescuers swept over them, swinging bats and quirts and ax handles.

"Arapahos! Counting coup! Just like we have always done!" Neiwoo watched her people touching but not harming the enemy. She was so proud! She jumped from the coach and danced like a girl.

The fight was a short one. The outlaws stood in a tight circle, like subdued cattle. Arapaho cavalry trotted around them. Then, as the dust-fog of thirty warhorses began to settle, out trotted a sweaty little gray mare. A left-handed Arapaho boy rode on her back, waving the Taker Man's black hat. My brother was smiling wide. I think that Flicka was smiling, too.

CHAPTER 24

Goodbye in a Good Way

The next day, the circle fully closed. Tasina Sa and Looking Glass were back home below the White Buttes. Neiwoo, Left Hand, and I were back near the canyon where her children, our parents, were both born and buried.

There was a celebration dance. After that, the last of the Fort Robinson Arapaho prepared to leave. They would live near the families of the rescued children in Wyoming. The stolen children would also circle back. Aunties and uncles brought them into their families at Fort Bob. The light in their young eyes returned. And soon they would travel the road to Wind River again.

CHAPTER 25

We Stayed

You know now that this horse-taming old man and this old lady are Left Hand and Sings in the Light. Neiwoo lived near Fort Robinson with us until she was very, very old. Always, she was singing, praying, and encouraging us in the Northern Arapaho way. She told us the stories of the Arapaho until our hearts and memories were full of them. She forgave the Takers, but always wondered about the green-eyed girl and her little ones after they were taken East.

Neiwoo told, but mostly showed, us how to be Arapaho from the time we were babies. She was a praying woman, like her people. Like her people, she was unafraid of danger. She was kind and generous. She showed compassion, always. Above all, she taught this truth—*that good will return to those who do good.* That is what Left Hand and I remember most. Good followed Neiwoo like a circle made of light. She sang in that light and gave her name to me.

We Arapaho know that the circle is sacred. That the sound of the round drum is our heartbeat. When we are near the drum, we feel its strong vibrations in our hearts. The songs sung around the drum carry our stories and our prayers. Neiwoo, Left Hand, and Sings in the Light saw that our circle was sacred like the drum, and that we would stay where we had returned, in a quiet canyon near the White Buttes.

VOCABULARY

Arapaho—In this book, this term refers to the Northern Arapaho, a Plains Indian, horse-culture tribe of North America.

arroyo—A shallow canyon that is made by running water, but is dry most of the time.

bedroll—A portable combination of sleeping pad, blankets, and waterproof cover.

beeves—A cowboy term for beef cattle.

bounty—A reward paid for the capture of animals or people.

covered wagon—A large wagon for transporting goods. It is covered by an arch-supported canvas.

ford—To cross a river or stream. Or, a place where it is possible to ford a stream.

halter—A rope or strap harness placed on a horse's head so that a person can lead the animal.

Hereford—A reddish-brown, white-faced breed of beef cattle.

hobbles—A rope or strap used to tie the feet of a horse loosely together so that it cannot walk away.

hohou (ha-HO)—"Thank you" in the Northern Arapaho language.

Hole in the Wall—A rocky place in eastern Wyoming, once used as an outlaw hideout.

lead rope—A rope that can be

attached to a halter and used to lead a horse.

Medicine Wheel—A sacred symbol of American Indian cultures.

niioo3o (Nee-AW-tha)—The Northern Arapaho word for "spider." Also means "White Man."

Oglala Lakota—The Oglala are a clan of the Lakota tribe of Plains Indians.

parfleche—A rawhide box made to hold and transport small objects.

quirt—A short, sturdy riding whip.

Red Cloud Indian Agency—Headquarters of the Indian Agent of the United States Government to the Oglala

Lakota tribe. Camp Robinson (later Fort Robinson) was a U.S. Army post located nearby. In 1878, the Red Cloud Agency was moved to its present location in South Dakota and renamed Pine Ridge Indian Reservation.

six-shooter—Cowboy and Indian term for a pistol with a revolving chamber holding six bullets.

stagecoach—A horse-drawn coach for carrying passengers.

tipi—A large tent or lodge used by many American Indian tribes.

wash (n.)—See *arroyo*. Usually a dry stream channel several feet deep and with steep walls.

Winchester—A lever-action repeating rifle used from the 1870s through today. Associated with cowboys, Indians, and the Old West.

wohei (WA-hay)—"All right" or "well done" in the Northern Arapaho language.

ARAPAHO LANGUAGE GUIDE

DICTIONARY OF THE NORTHERN ARAPAHO LANGUAGE (REVISED)

1998

Revised from the original
Dictionary of Contemporary Arapaho Usage (1983),
compiled by Zdenek Salzmann and the Arapaho Language and Culture Commission

Revision was completed through collaboration of:

The Arapaho Language and Culture Commission

Arapahoe School

The Northern Arapaho Tribe

Jeffrey Anderson

ARAPAHO ALPHABET

LETTERS:

b c e h i k n o s 3 t u w x y '

VOWELS:

SHORT VOWELS: are the basic building blocks of other vowels.

e is a short vowel sound like the "e" in the English word "bet."

i is a short vowel that sounds like the "i" in the English term "bit."

o is similar to the vowel sound in the English word "got."

u is like the English short "u" sound in "put."

LONG VOWELS: are the vowels listed above, but.held longer.

Long vowels are indicated by the doubling or tripling of the same vowel sounds above or combinations (diphthongs) of different vowel sounds.

ee is close in sound to the English short "a" sound as in "bat."

ii is similar to the long "e" in English, such as in "beet."

oo is much like the long "ah" sound as in "caught" or "fought,"

uu is a long "u" sound as in the English word "dude."

VOWEL COMBINATIONS (DIPTHONGS): are combinations of the short vowel sound put together.

ei is much the like the long "a" sound as in the English word "weight."

ou is a long "o" sound in English, as in "boat."

oe is similar to the long "i" sound in English, as in "bite."

ie is rare in Arapaho, but is made by first saying the short "i" sound as in "bit" and then the short "e" sound as in "bet," listed above.

TRIPLE VOWELS: are extra long vowels or diphthongs that are held even longer and usually have a stress at the beginning and end. For example the word "booo" is a long "oo" sound with an added and stressed "o" sound on the end. Usually the stress is on the first vowel and the last.

eee is an extra long "e" or three "e's" put together.

iii is an extra long "i." or three "i's" put together..

ooo is an extra long "o", or three "o's" put together

uuu is an extra long "u" or three "u's" put together.

eii is an "ei" sound with an "i" sound added to the end.

oee is an "oe" sound held somewhat longer.

ouu is an "ou" sound with a "u" added to the end.

CONSONANTS:

b is slightly less voiced (less sound) than the English "b" at the beginning and in the middle of words, but like a "p" (unvoiced, no sound) at the end.

c is between an English "j" and "ch." It is more like a "j" at the beginning of words.

h is like the English "h," but when at the end of a word or syllable it is breathed (air is forced out slightly)

k is a blend of "k" and "g," but more like "g" at the beginning of words, and more like "k" at the end.

n is more or less the same as the English "n."

s is like the English "s" as in "sea," but is never like a "z" sound as in "trees."

t sounds like an English "d," as in "dot" at the beginning of words, but more like a "t" elsewhere.

3 is similar to the unvoiced "th" sound in English, as in "thin," but never like the voiced "th" sound as in "the" or "that."

w is the same as "w" in water, but in Arapaho you must also make the "w" rounded lip shape when it is at the end, as in the Arapaho word woow, meaning "now"

x does not have a similar sound in English, but is like the "ch" sound in German, as in "ich" or "machen"

y is the same as the English "y," but must be shaped with the mouth at the end of words, too.

' is a glottal stop. It is made by closing the opening at the back of the throat, as in the Arapaho word ho' for "dirt."